This Book
Belongs

to

DORCAS PORKUS

by Tasha Tudor

HENRY Z. WALCK, INCORPORATED
New York

J
T

CALLIGRAPHY BY HILDA SCOTT

A Story
for
Ellen and Berty

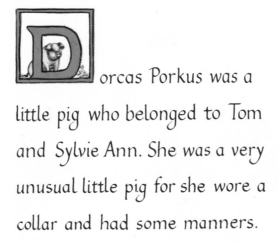orcas Porkus was a little pig who belonged to Tom and Sylvie Ann. She was a very unusual little pig for she wore a collar and had some manners.

ne day their Mimmsy was giving a church quilting bee. She explained that the elderly ladies might not like a tame pig, and asked Sylvie Ann and Tom to keep Dorcas Porkus out of sight.

o when the guests arrived they decided to take Dorcas to call on Grandmimmsy. But just as they were starting Dorcas lay down in a very muddy mud puddle.

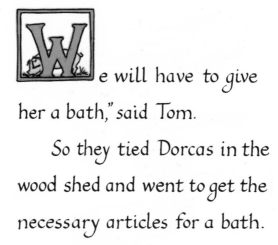e will have to give her a bath," said Tom.

So they tied Dorcas in the wood shed and went to get the necessary articles for a bath.

ylvie Ann got her
Mimmsy's laundry tub and
a piece of soap.

om went to get two
buckets of water.

Alexander the Gander came
to see who was using the well;
he was very annoying and
made a lot of noise.

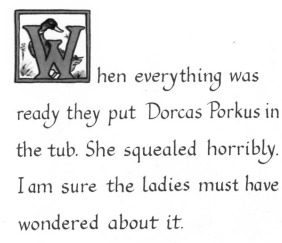hen everything was ready they put Dorcas Porkus in the tub. She squealed horribly. I am sure the ladies must have wondered about it.

ll of a sudden Dorcas
knew she didn't want a bath! She gave one jump, and over went the tub and the buckets and Sylvie Ann.

Unfortunately the shed door was open, leading right into the kitchen, and that is where Dorcas went just as fast as she could go!

ust at that moment Mimmsy opened the parlor door and Dorcas Porkus ran right into the middle of the quilting party. You can imagine how dreadful that must have been!

ut even worse! She dashed beneath the skirts of Mrs. Bartram, the minister's wife, and tried to hide!!

inally Dorcas escaped through the front door, and ran to the hay barn, where Tom and Sylvie Ann found her hiding in an overturned barrel.

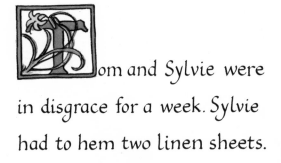om and Sylvie were in disgrace for a week. Sylvie had to hem two linen sheets.

nd Tom had to clean the chicken house.

They felt better next Sunday when Mrs. Bartram gave them peppermints and said it was the liveliest quilting bee she had ever attended.

s for Dorcas Porkus,
she went to live in the pig yard,
where she lies in all the mud
puddles she likes, and tells the
other pigs what dreadful things
soap and clean water and church
quilting bees are.

the end

Date Due